To Owen and Wyatt, my winners

—S.F.

To Jamey and my three dogs that keep me
company all day: Samurai, Hansel, and Jinx

—E.T.

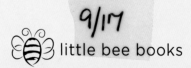

An imprint of Bonnier Publishing USA
251 Park Avenue South, New York, NY 10010
Text copyright © 2017 by Sue Fliess
Illustrations copyright © 2017 by Edwardian Taylor
Manufactured in China   LEO 1116
First Edition
2 4 6 8 10 9 7 5 3 1
ISBN 978-1-4998-0237-5
Library of Congress Cataloging-in-Publication Data
Names: Fliess, Sue, author. | Taylor, Edwardian, illustrator.
Title: Race! / by Sue Fliess; illustrated by Edwardian Taylor.
Description: First Edition. | New York: Little Bee Books, [2017] |
Summary: Cars line up for the Winner's Cup, and with one car smaller than the rest, they all
speed down mountains, by waterfalls, through tunnels, and past landslides to the finish line.
Subjects: | CYAC: Stories in rhyme. | Automobiles—Fiction. | Automobile racing—Fiction.
Classification: LCC PZ8.3.F642 Rac 2017 | DDC [E]—dc23
LC record available at https://lccn.loc.gov/2016014967
Identifiers: LCCN 2016014967

littlebeebooks.com
bonnierpublishingusa.com

RACE!

by **Sue Fliess**

illustrated by **Edwardian Taylor**

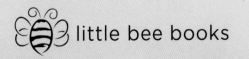 little bee books

Race cars!
Line up!

Who will take the
Winner's Cup?

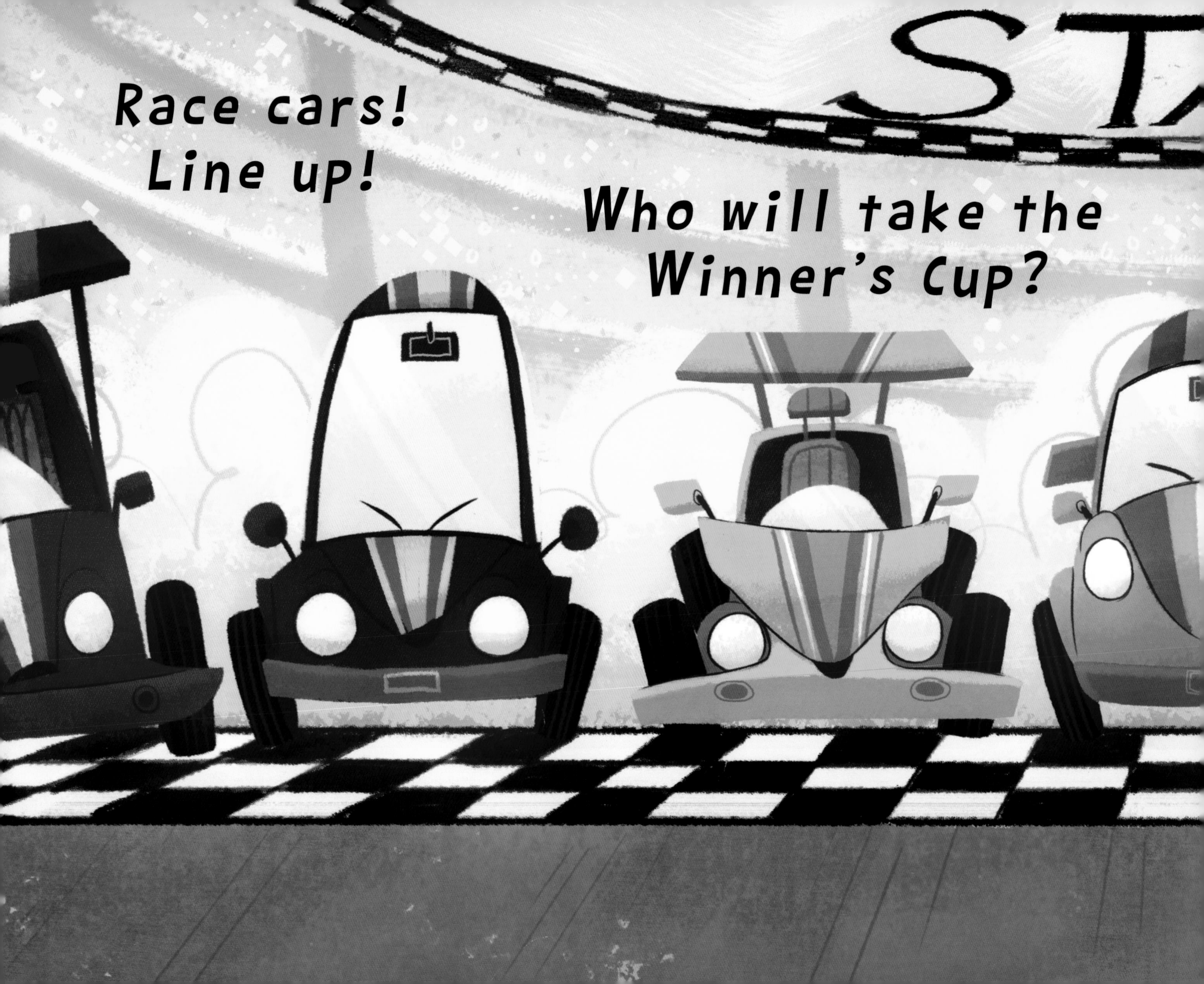

"Rev your engines...
GO GO GO!"

ZOOM! VROOM!
SPEED! STEER!

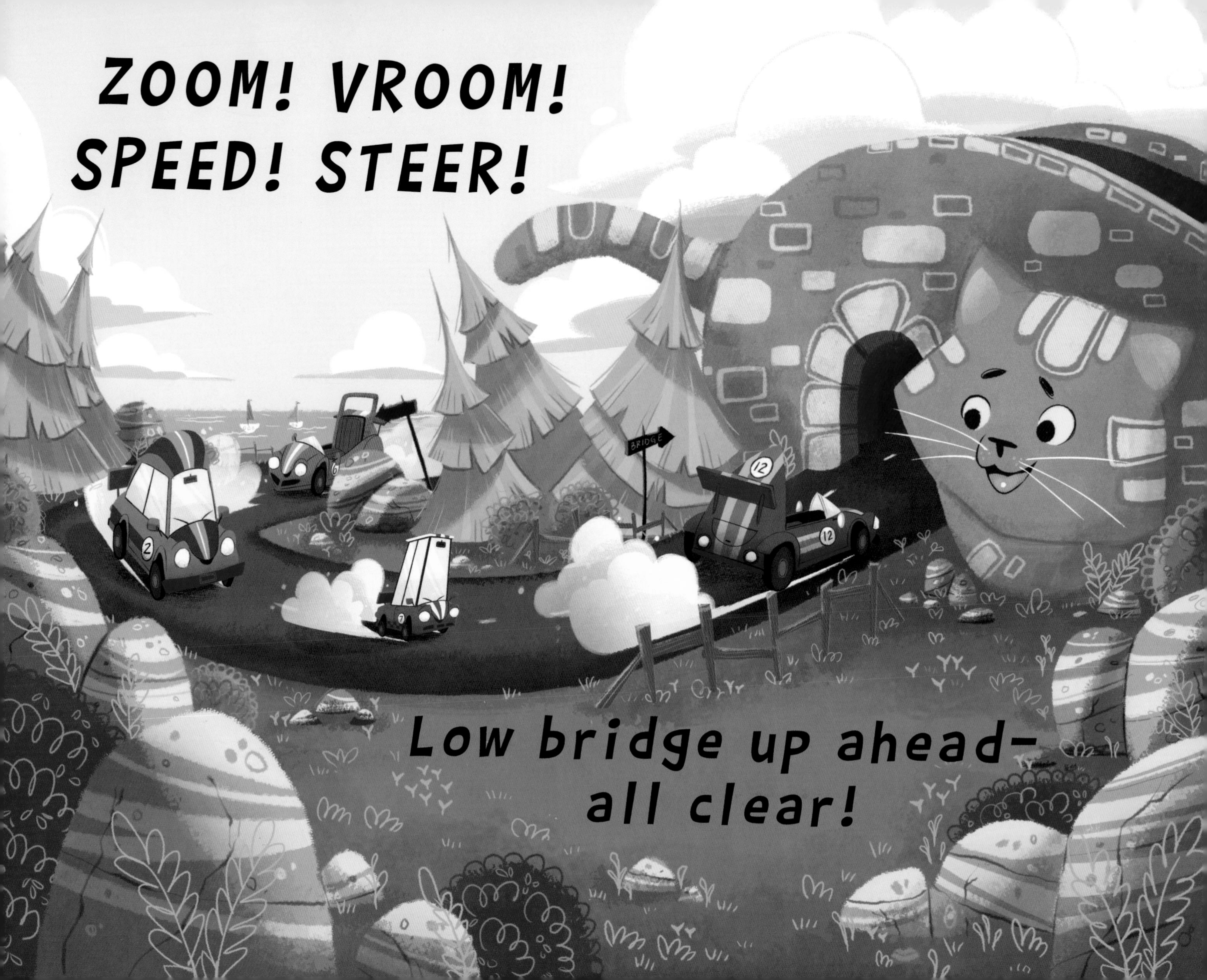

Low bridge up ahead—
all clear!

BLAST! BANK! TWIST! TURN!

Down the mountain, tires burn!

SKID! SCREECH!
Close call...

watch out for
the waterfall!

SLIP! SLAM!
SQUEAL! SOAR!

Through the tunnel!
Thunder! Roar!

DART! DIVE!
SWERVE! SWAY!
Turtle crossing...

save the day !

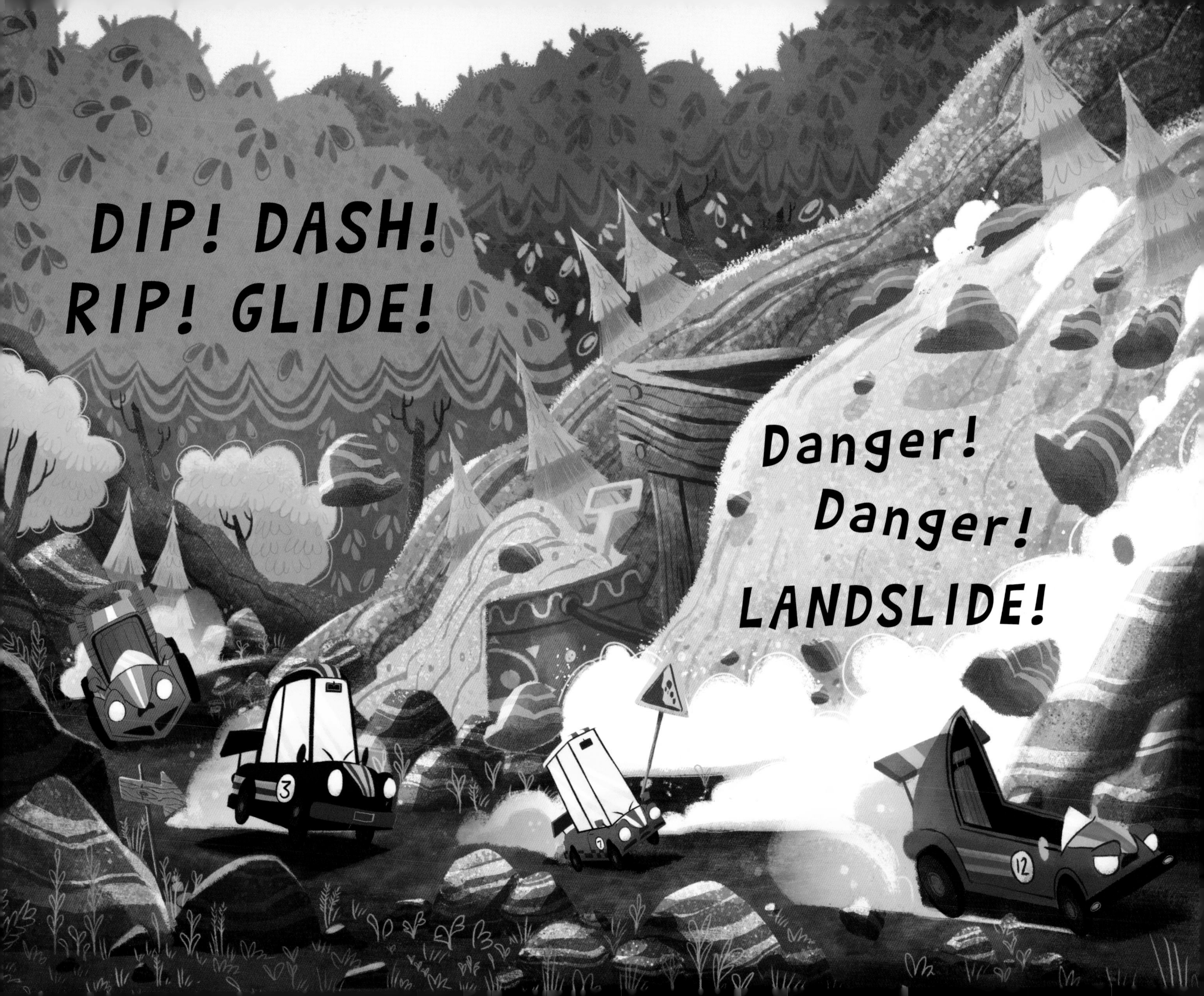

DIP! DASH!
RIP! GLIDE!

Danger!
Danger!
LANDSLIDE!

Ramp up,
fast lane...

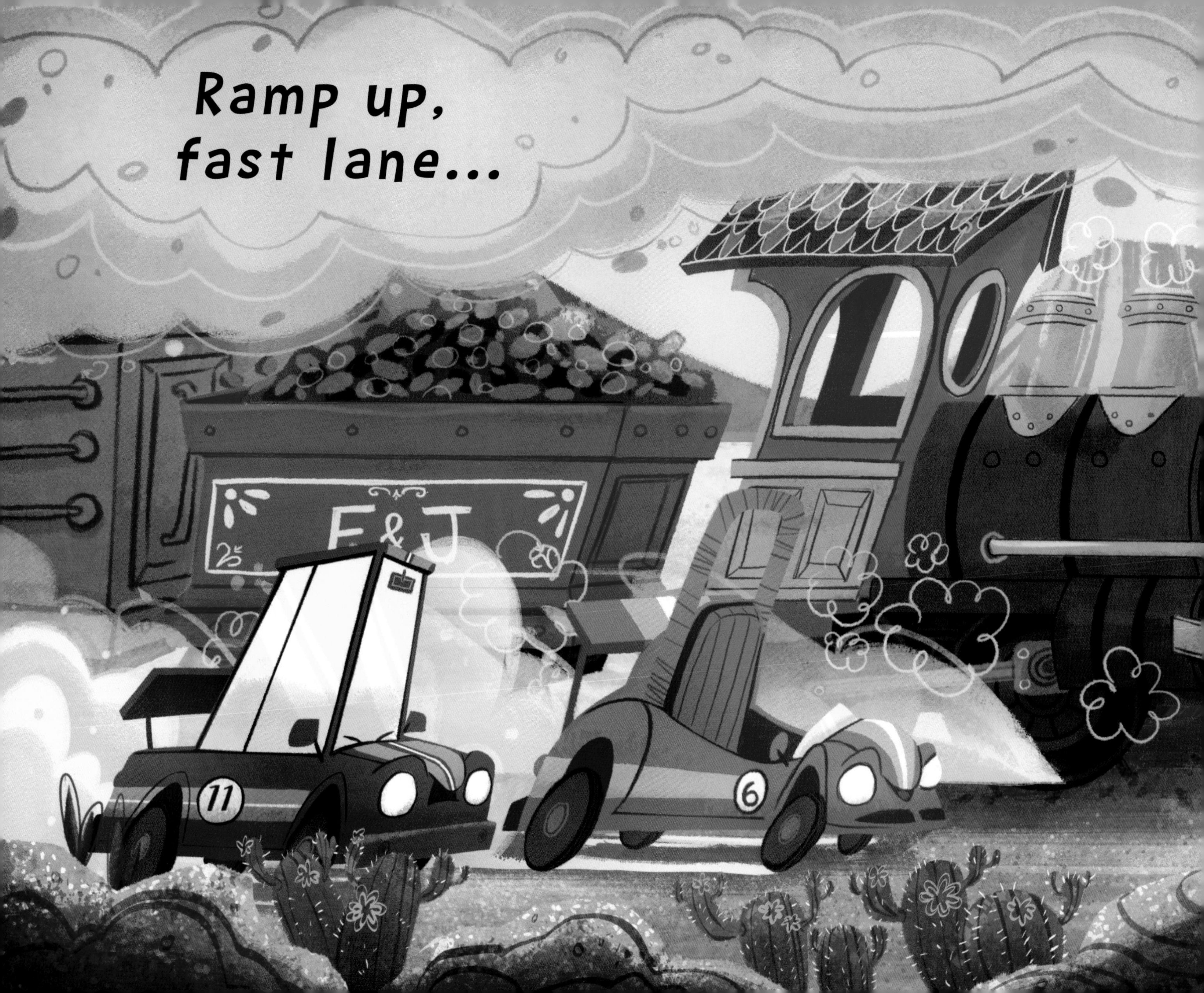

try to beat the moving train!

WHAM! BAM!
BONK! CONK!

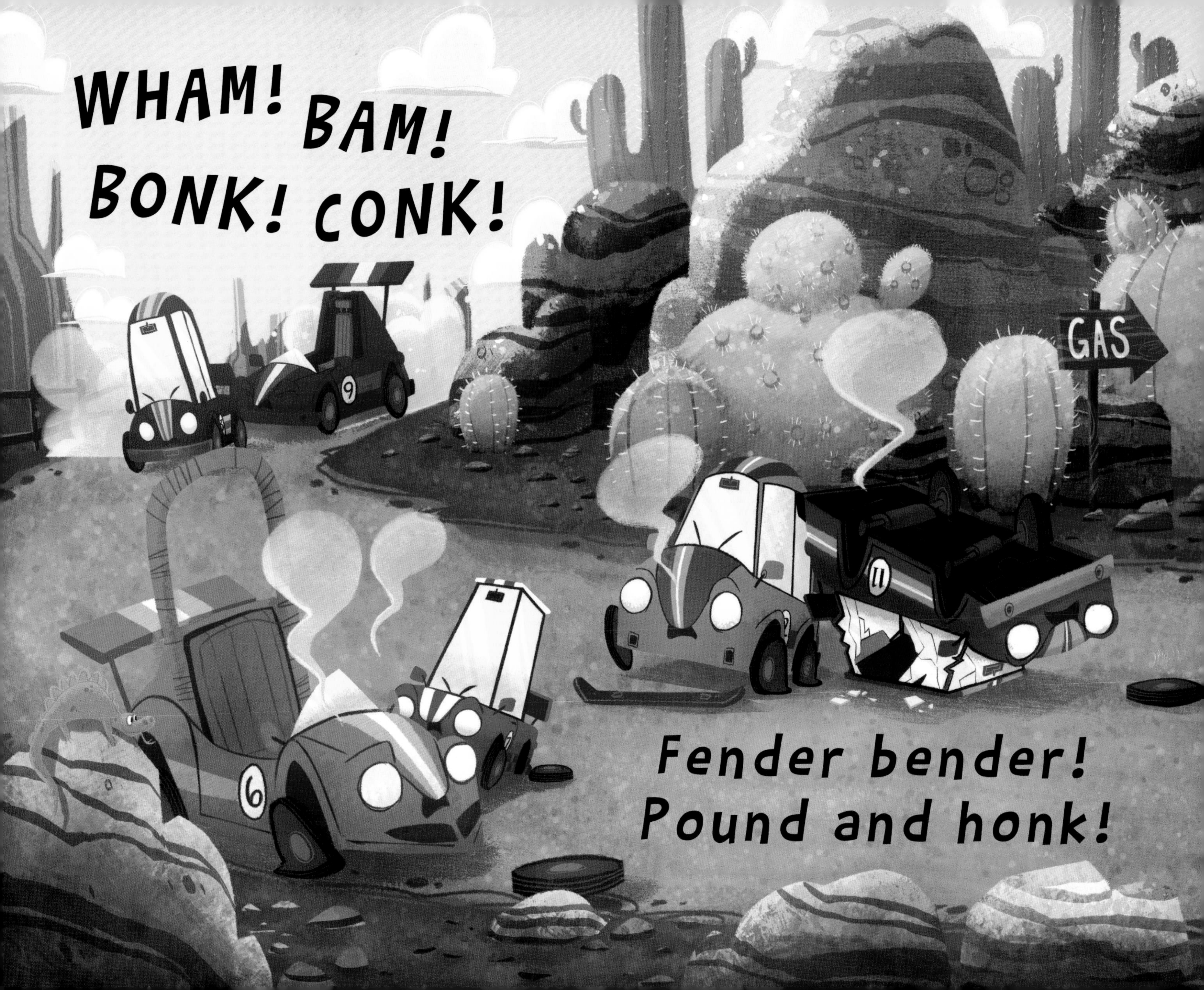

Fender bender!
Pound and honk!

PIT STOP!
Quick fix–

zipping back
into the mix.....

JOLT! FLY!
BOLT! PASS!

Take a shortcut
through the grass.

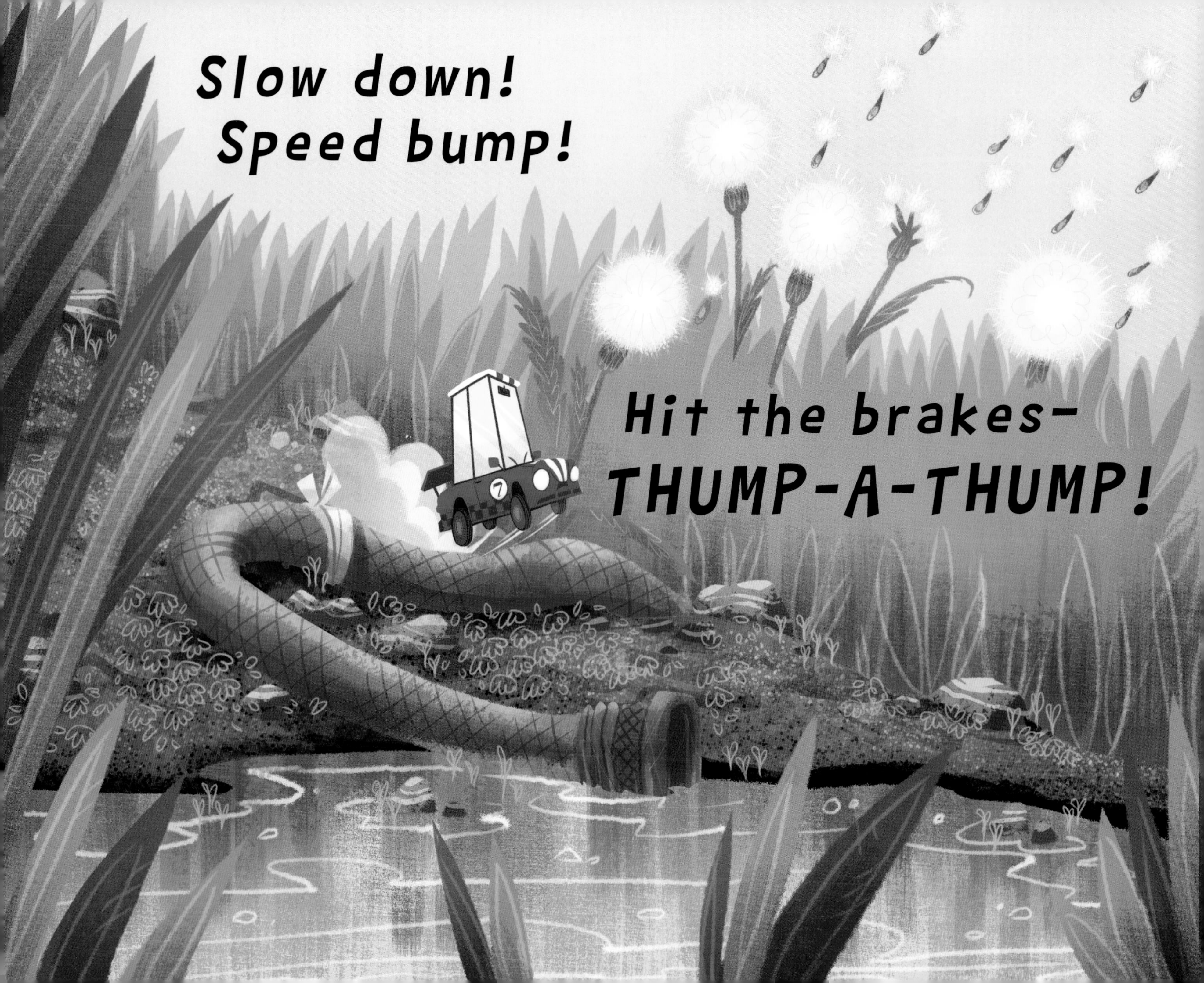

Slow down!
Speed bump!

Hit the brakes–
THUMP-A-THUMP!

FULL THROTTLE!
TOP SPEED!

Small car jumps
into the lead!

Home stretch,
tight race—

launching into
outer space.....

"Maxwell...time for snack."

One more trip around the track.

WHIZ! WHOOSH!
RUSH! SPIN!

Small car crosses for the win!

"All right...

fuel up for the race tonight!"

"Great job, small car!

You're my favorite racing star."